High on the S...

An
Intergenerational
Adventure
into the
Mountains
of Oregon

BONNIE SHUMAKER

HIGH ON THE SADDLE

Published by Paloma Books

(An imprint of L&R Publishing, LLC)

Paloma Books

PO Box 3531

Ashland, OR 97520

www.palomabooks.com

Cover & Interior Design: L. Redding

Cover & Interior Illustrations: Elecia Beebe

ISBN: 978-1-55571-923-4

Library of Congress CIP information available from the publisher on request.

Printed and Bound in the USA

10 9 8 7 6 5 4 3 2 1

For Rosemary Kemper who introduced me to Saddle Mountain and encouraged the writing of this book, and to my mother who taught me to love and explore both words and nature.

"It's just not fair," I grumble, running out the door. I don't exactly slam the door, but I close it hard enough so no one can miss how I feel. My words trail behind me: "It's ONLY a stupid game. What's the big deal!?" After I say that, I feel heat rise to my face and my eyes start burning. I know embarrassing tears are coming, so I escape.

What brought this on was the announcement that my sister, Penny, had made the Summer All-Star Soccer Team. I am expected to share in the excitement, but I just can't. Penny is twelve, three years older than I am, and her nickname is "Penny Perfect." She has lots of friends, does better in school, and always seems to be the first and best in everything. "It's just not fair," I repeat.

I stomp towards the barn, kicking up dust and gravel along the way. Then I see Henry, our ram, by his gate. I dry my eyes and stop to tell him my troubles. "Henry, why can't I ever do anything good?" I ask, as I hold his head between my hands. Henry wiggles over so his back is presented for a good scratching. "Oh, I see," I reply, "I AM good for what itches," so I give his back a good working over, especially around his neck. Henry rewards me by curling back his lip in a happy sheep smile. "You silly old ram," I tease, kissing him on the nose. I gaze past him to the pasture where the rest of the sheep are grazing. Their half-grown lambs leap and chase each other around the pasture. I think back to lambing time this winter. I love to get the newborn lambs and their mothers into the pens, put iodine on their belly buttons, and help them get milk. Once, I saved a lamb's life! I heard a really sad "baa" and found a just-born lamb stuck behind a water tub. I picked it up and got both the lamb and its mother into a pen.

Just then, my dogs Misty and Honey come wagging over. Honey holds a stick in her mouth. "Shall we go for a walk?" I ask. Their bouncy, tail-wagging response leaves no doubt. After locking the pasture gate behind us, we all run pell-mell down the hill to the pond. The dogs splash in ready to play their "old dog, young dog" fetching game. Misty swims out to fetch the stick I throw. Then Honey takes it from her at the pond's edge and brings it back to me for another throw. When Misty was a pup, Honey taught her everything a dog should know, but now that she is old, she lets let Misty do most of the work.

After a while, the dogs and I tire of the game. They follow me along the edge of the pond while I examine the frog eggs in the cattails at the shallow end. The tiny tadpoles are wiggling in their jelly-like case almost ready to hatch. I'll have to come back soon to check on them. I watch as a kind of salamander, called a newt, strolls along the grass. I love this critter's shiny little eyes and bright orange belly. It doesn't move fast, but it knows where it is going as it heads toward the pond. I move a rock out of the way that looks like it is in the newt's path. "That should help you, little one," I say. Then I watch as it slips into the pond. As it swims away, its body bends from side to side leaving a zig-zag pattern on top of the water.

I've been told that I have a special way with nature. People say I inherited this from my Grandma. Maybe that is why Grandma and I are so close. Thinking about Grandma, I call the dogs and head back up the hill to her house. She lives on the same farm as we do in the little house up the path. Grandpa lived there too, before he died when I was just five. I don't want Grandma to know about the upset at my house, and I'm feeling better now anyway, so I greet her with a much happier subject.

After giving my special "shave and a haircut, six bits" knock, I push open the door to find Grandma washing the lunch dishes. I greet her with, "Should we check out the wild blackberries?"

"Sounds like a winner to me," Grandma replies. "There were a few ripe ones when we checked last week. Why don't you grab that dishtowel and help me dry these things? Then I'll get on my walking shoes while you get the blackberry sticks and buckets we left in the shed. If we find enough berries, we can make a pie for tonight."

After the dishes are done, I head outside for the sticks and buckets. When Grandma comes out she calls, "Let's go, Puppy Dog."

"After you, Grandmother Eagle," I reply with a smile. Grandma calls me "Puppy Dog" because whenever we go for a walk, I get excited and run ahead to see what's new and then trot back to report the news—just like any pup you ever knew. Grandma is "Grandmother Eagle" because her alert eyes and ears are always open for little things like mushrooms, wild flowers, birds, and animal tracks.

There is one thing you can count on with Grandma and me: If one of us gets a hankering to go for a walk, the other will find a way to go, too. We don't care about the weather. Rainy walks are a favorite. That's when the mushrooms appear and the spider webs are easy to spot as they shine with wetness. Grandma never says to stay out of the puddles as we splash and laugh and explore. Grandma is smart about lots of things. She knows the names of wildflowers, mushrooms, and birds, and what isn't in her head, she looks up in books. She teaches me much of what she knows. She says I have taught her lots, too. Grandma says there's no end to learning. That's for sure.

The blackberries we are searching for are the early summer, ground trailing kind that a lot of people ignore because they are small and hard to find. But our family knows that their flavor is the secret to the very best pies. We search in the recently logged land between the old stumps and young trees. As we walk along the trail, Grandma spies some tiny "inside-out" flowers. "Looks like they climbed on the stem backward, doesn't it? Oh, look at this! Here's one entwined around a new little fir tree, decorating it like a Christmas tree." The dogs and I run over to share in Grandma's delightful discovery.

Further on, we spy berry vines snaking out onto the trail. We follow them into the woods and find a bunch of berries growing over an old stump. The berries are sun-warmed and delicious. We pick the sweetest, blackest ones, then push aside vines with our sticks to spot more berries further off the trail. I'm glad I wore long pants, shoes, and socks. These blackberries live up to their nickname of "ankle-grabbers." I also reach carefully through the vines to get the berries so the stickers don't get me. The bottoms of our pails are almost covered when I ask, "Have you heard what the weather's going to be tomorrow?"

"Yes, I have, and it looks promising, sunshine all the way to the coast," Grandma says. Grandma and I have planned something special. We are going to hike Saddle Mountain—to the very top. Grandma says that from there, on a clear day, you can see the Columbia River meet the Pacific Ocean, and all the shoreline clear down to Nehalem Bay—about fifty miles!

Grandma hasn't climbed Saddle Mountain in lots of years. I never have. It's a long hike and really steep in places. Not so you need mountain climbing gear or anything, but Grandma remembers it being a long, hard climb. This summer, we decided I'm old enough, and Grandma's not too old; and together, we're going to do it.

After an hour, we have enough berries for a pie, and head for Grandma's house. First, we make the piecrust. Grandma reminds me to roll out the piecrust from the center to keep it round, to sprinkle flour on the breadboard, and turn the crust often so it won't stick. We add the berries to the bottom crust and sprinkle sugar, flour and pieces of butter on top. Now comes my favorite part; weaving the strips of dough to make a crisscross top crust. While we work, Grandma asks, "Is your backpack ready for tomorrow?"

"I've got everything in except the lunch, and I need to fill my water bottles," I answer. "I used the list we made last week of what we need. I've got it memorized." My eyes look up as I search my brain. I count off the fingers of both hands and two more and recite: "Lunch, water bottles, energy snacks, compass, space blanket, bug spray, sunscreen, matches, first aid kit, camera, binoculars, and wild flower chart."

"Good job," says Grandma. "I'll carry the lunch in my pack. You've got the rest."

In about an hour, our cooking mess is cleaned up and Grandma lifts the pie out of the oven, bubbling hot and golden brown. The whole house smells delicious. Grandma comes to dinner at our house, and the pie is a big hit. Fortunately, nothing was said about Penny's soccer team or my behavior.

The next morning, I set my alarm early and eat breakfast with Dad before he goes to work. Mom and Penny are still sleeping.

Dad asks, "Well, are you ready for the big climb?"

"I think so," I reply. "I hope we can make it clear to the top."

"I'm betting on you," says Dad. "You and your Grandma can do just about anything. I can still taste that delicious pie from last night. Yum!"

After breakfast, I check my backpack for the umpteenth time, put it on and walk up the path to see if Grandma is ready.

"What a beautiful morning!" she says when she hears my knock, and I open the door. "I feel like climbing a mountain today. How about you?"

"Yes Ma'am," I say and salute her like a soldier. Grandma is putting the finishing touches on the lunch. Ham and cheese sandwiches, chips, cherries off our tree, and even two pieces of blackberry pie in a crushproof container. The boxed drinks we're taking have been in the freezer so they will keep the sandwiches cool on the hike. With luck, the juice will thaw just in time to drink it on the mountaintop.

I remind Grandma, "Don't forget forks for the pie," and she packs the forks and the rest of the lunch in her backpack. She lifts the two packs and declares they weigh about the same. "These should do nicely," she says. "And they're not too heavy either." Both our packs have two water bottle holders built in, and before setting the bottles there, Grandma adds ice cubes to the water so it will stay cold.

Finally, we're off! Driving over the mountains toward the coast, we watch the sky, and the weather stays exciting! At the highest point on the highway, I strain my eyes forward and then wiggle excitedly as I point out the window. "Look, Grandma, it's just what we ordered! Blue sky and no fog or clouds trying to push in from the ocean. Nothing will spoil our view!"

Soon, we take the Saddle Mountain turnoff. I want to be there right now, but we still have seven miles to go on a skinny, twisty road before we finally arrive at the trailhead parking lot. It is only nine o'clock, and there is just one other car here. We planned this early start to give us plenty of time to take it slow on our hike and rest when we need to. There is a restroom at the parking lot, which is a good idea since the hike will take most of the day.

"Look, Grandma," I cry as I point to where the trail starts. "That looks like a map of the trail." I'm right. The trailhead sign has a map, but I am too antsy to study it for long, so I do my Puppy Dog thing and scamper ahead.

Right away, I get worried. The trail really is steep, my legs are already tired, and I'm out of breath. I've got a pain in my side, and we've only just begun. As I stop to wait for Grandma, I remember how she taught me to find a round rock to spit under when I get a pain in my side from going too fast. You have to find the perfect round rock, pick it up and then spit right where the rock was. It takes a few spits to land exactly in that place, but when I hit the mark, that pain is gone, sure as anything. It works every time.

When Grandma catches up, she is out of breath, too. I am relieved to hear her say, "Well, Puppy Dog. I'm glad you stopped here. I remember now how steep this trail starts out, but if I'm not mistaken, it levels out soon." Sure enough, after only one more rest on this steep part, we feel better as the trail changes. Now it uses switchbacks, which are like zig-zags that climb the mountain. They go across, turn, and go back again higher up.

Just before the trail turns at each switchback, you can barely see a little trail that goes straight up to the next level. I want to take this shortcut. "The trail gets wrecked when people take a shortcut before the switchback," Grandma points out. "Since the shortcuts go straight up, when the rains come, the water channels down them making ditches that can wash the trail away." That makes sense, so I make myself stay on the main trail.

The woods are beginning to open up more to the sky now, and it is getting warmer. We stop for a minute to stuff our jackets in our backpacks and put on sunscreen. Hiking again, I love the changing view at the end of each switchback showing how much higher we've come. At the end of one, when I look down, we seem so far above where we left our car. I also look up and see we still have a long way to go.

Grandma is beginning to find lots of wildflowers now, so I stay with her and use my own eagle eye to help spot them. We come to one open place that faces the sun where Grandma exclaims, "Look, here's 'Nature's bouquet.' She's put all these beautiful flowers together to complement each other."

Soon we start laughing at ourselves for all the times we say "Wow!" as we spot more beautiful "bouquets." Then we turn scientific as we use our wildflower chart to help us identify Indian Paintbrush, Cow Parsnip, Penstemon, Tiger Lily, Wild Hollyhock, Iris Flags, Columbine, and Larkspur. I take lots of pictures and experiment with the zoom lens on my camera to try for a close-up of the flowers. I remember the secret that Dad told me. Hold your camera really still, even for a second or two after taking the picture. I think I got some really good pictures.

After quite a bit more hiking, we come to a huge rock overlooking the valley far below. You can even see a bit of the ocean. "Is this the top?" I ask hopefully.

"This is the false summit," Grandma explains, "and one place where many people do stop. We will rest here and decide if we want to go on." It feels wonderful to take off our backpacks and sit down to have a drink from our still icy-cold water bottles and eat a snack.

We check out the view all around us. Grandma is peering through the binoculars when she points and says, "Do you see those two peaks in the distance? I'm going to call them 'Parentheses Mountains' because their tops are shaped with curves facing each other just

like the punctuation marks." She hands me the binoculars to scan the horizon. I grin when I spot the same mountains and agree that would be the perfect name for them.

On the edge of our big rock, another tall rock tower leans dangerously out over the valley. I tell Grandma, "I'm naming this 'Knob Top' because of the little rock sitting on top of the rock tower. It looks like one push from a giant's finger would send the whole thing tumbling down the mountain."

"I agree," Grandma replies. "It also looks like it's been here for thousands of years, defying the law of gravity." After about fifteen minutes, the food and rest have given us a second wind. I am pleased that my energy can return so fast. Grandma and I make the decision to go on.

We hike around a rocky side of the mountain and past a creek that burbles out of the rocks. Then Grandma points out a side trail, a gravelly scoop out on a ridge that looks kind of like a saddle. I ask Grandma if this trail is where Saddle Mountain got its name. "I don't think so. It got its name from the view from Astoria across Young's Bay where you can see the whole mountain. This must be the "mini-saddle.""

We spot some people on this side-trail who are actually walking this saddle. "Shall we do that?" I ask.

"Not this time," says Grandma. "We've still got our goal to meet and probably shouldn't waste any of our second wind." So, we go forward, me first again.

I pretend I'm a famous explorer, striding along the path like a conquering hero, tall and brave, ready to claim this mountain for my own. Coming around a corner, I gasp when I spy a mama deer and her twin spotted fawns grazing in an open meadow. They startle and thrill me at the same time. Instantly, I crouch down to become small and hidden, so I won't scare them. I signal to Grandma as she rounds the same corner, and she immediately knows to be quiet and still. Her eyes follow where I point. She gives a small cry of delight and crouches down next to me. Together we smile and enter the enchantment. The deer seem to see us as they lift their heads, but they don't act afraid. They keep walking toward us as they eat, until finally they turn off into the woods.

"Wow!" I say, practically bursting with excitement. "Have you ever seen that here before?"

"No," Grandma answers. "This is a first. Those deer must have been put there especially for us."

The thrill of seeing the deer stays with us as we map out the remainder of our hike. "There's the summit," says Grandma as she points across a valley to where the forest and meadow give way to a rocky climb to the very top of Saddle Mountain. "I'd love to measure that distance 'as the crow flies,'" Grandma continues, "but since we don't have wings and feathers, we have go down into the valley and then up the other side." It is a tiring thought for two already tired hikers, but the day has already been so special. The sky is still blue, and the promised view awaits.

As we begin our steep climb down into the valley, we see giant wooden steps off to the side of the trail. They were built to protect both hikers and the trail. Grandma laughingly remembers these steps from a previous climb. She comments, "These steps are so big, a Paul Bunyan of the Forestry Department must have built them." I see what she means. I would feel very short-legged trying to climb down them. Right alongside the steps, however, it looks like someone had a better idea for this steep part. There is something kind of like a chain-link fence lying on the ground. The chain-links keep your feet from slipping and there is a cable to hold onto, too. We decide this is the better way, and it works.

The climb up the other side is even steeper. "Connecting these logs with cables to make a ladder for our feet was a good idea," Grandma remarks. "And these sagging cables give us something to hold onto as we pull ourselves up." I am glad I wore hiking boots with good traction. Even so, I slip a couple of times, but holding onto the cable keeps me from falling far or getting hurt.

Grandma cautions, "Don't hurry; we just have to take it slow and easy for now." This is the most dangerous part of the hike. We concentrate on not falling and don't look around much at the view. The ground seems to be nothing but rocks, but we still see wildflowers blooming here. Amazing!

Finally, we drag ourselves up the last bit of trail by holding on to the cable and we're here—at the top! I walk on shaky legs to the edge. I can't believe how high we are and how much we can see. There is a fence here to keep excited hikers from falling. I hold on to it as I try to see everything at once.

The breeze on the mountaintop is stronger and much cooler with no trees around, but it feels good after our hard climb. "I'm sure glad this fence is here," I tell Grandma. "We're so high, I'm almost dizzy."

Grandma hugs me tightly with one arm and with the other points out the Astoria Bridge that crosses the Columbia River where it widens into the Pacific Ocean. My eyes follow her arm as she points out the shoreline clear down to Nehalem Bay. "That's fifty miles of coastline you're seeing," says Grandma. "Can you see how the waves show bits of white as they break along the shore?"

"I see them," I reply. "They look so tiny. And look at the forest below us. Those must be roads we see. They look like tiny ribbons of thread."

"That's a managed forest you're seeing," instructs Grandma, "where trees are grown as a crop. It takes forty to sixty years for a tree to get big enough to make lumber. You can tell the young trees and the older ones by their light green or dark green color. In Oregon, when trees are cut, forest owners must replant within two years. See the brown areas? Those are recent cuts. There are probably new trees in them already, they're just too small for us to see from our bird's-eye view. Deer and elk like these open places. Other animals and birds like the young forest. We just hiked through the Saddle Mountain State Natural Area, over 3,200 acres of older forest that other animals and birds require."

Speaking of our birds-eye view, we see some birds actually flying below us! They ride the air currents as they swoop and dive. "It looks like they're having as much fun as we are," I say.

Grandma grabs my arm excitedly and points out one particular bird. "I'm pretty sure that's a Marbled Murrelet. It is rare to see them. They live mostly at sea, but fly inland to lay eggs and hatch babies this time of year. They need an older forest like what we've hiked through on Saddle Mountain."

That strong wind feels colder now, and we put on our jackets. There is actually a picnic table here to rest our weary bones while we eat our lunch. We wonder how both the fence and the picnic table got way up here. It would be really hard to carry them up the trail. We wonder if maybe they were brought in by helicopter. We chuckle at that idea, but maybe it is true.

The frozen juice boxes that Grandma packed are still a little frozen, kind of like a slushy, and taste delicious. As we eat, we get up from the picnic table a lot to check out the view and take pictures. I try to express the way I am feeling inside. "I feel kind of like I did when we saw the deer. Proud and strong to have made it to the top, but also as tiny as an ant compared to all the beautiful things around me. How can I feel big and small at the same time?"

"I don't know, but I feel it too," says Grandma. "I think that's the feeling that makes us want to take care of places like this, like picking up our trash and not harming the trail, as well as enjoying its beauty."

As we finish our lunch, I decide to tell Grandma about the way I acted yesterday when Penny made the All-Star Team. "I feel bad about it now. I'm sure I hurt Penny's feelings. I know Mom says I should be happy for other people and not be jealous, but sometimes, I just can't help it."

"It's not always easy being the younger one," says Grandma. "You'll figure out a way to make it up to her." Grandma has a special way of saying just the right thing with only a few words.

We stay a little longer congratulating each other on our successful hike and making plans for other hikes, until that cold wind sends us back down the mountain to the comfort of the woods. The first rocky part is even scarier going downhill, so I go slow and hold on really tight to the cable. Once we get back into the woods, the rest seems easy.

As we meet hikers going up the trail, I greet them with a happy smile and ask, "Have you ever hiked Saddle Mountain before?" I tell them that this is my first time, and it was great. They should look for deer in the meadow and a Marbled Murrelet at the top. It's fun to now be the expert. The sun is still shining, so even these late-comers should be able to see the great view.

Finally, our tired bodies welcome the end of the trail, and the comfort of the car feels like heaven. On the way home, we don't talk much. Behind my closed eyes, I see our hike all over again, and I feel so happy. An idea comes to me for a congratulation card to make for Penny. I'll draw my dark-haired sister in her soccer uniform kicking a goal. For the soccer ball, I'll use one of the stickers from my collection. I'll also add kitty stickers. Penny loves kittens. I'll write the words "Congratulations, Penny" and "Love, Me" on the card. I'll tell her I'm sorry for the way I acted. Maybe Penny would even like to go with me to hike Saddle Mountain someday. I also imagine more hikes with Grandma. Maybe a long time from now I'll take my own kids and grandkids on lots of hikes, so I can teach them like Grandma teaches me. It has been a very good day.

☙❧

S addle Mountain is a double-peaked saddle of pillow basalt rising 3,290 feet out of the surrounding forest. It forms the highest peak in the north Coast Range and the highest in Northwest Oregon.

Saddle Mountain State Natural Area claims 3,226 acres and is cherished for its hiking trails, wildflowers and breathtaking scenery. On a clear day, the panoramic view from the 3,290-foot summit shows the sweep of the Columbia River as it enters the sea, miles of Pacific shoreline, and on the eastern horizon, the Cascade Mountains in Oregon and Washington. The rigorous 2.5-mile hike with an elevation gain of 1,650 feet is difficult in spots and is recommended for experienced hikers. Weather conditions can change rapidly, bringing wind and rain year-round, so wear appropriate footwear and clothing.

About the Author

As a child, I was led by my mother's hand to discover the many delights of nature. In the various places we lived in the West while I was growing up, my mother always found trails to hike and trailing blackberries to pick to make the very best pies. These skills have been passed down through the generations.

Many years ago, a friend invited me to hike to the summit of Saddle Mountain. The hike was challenging, but the sky was clear, the wildflowers were in all their glory, and I was hooked. I have repeated this hike many times, including sharing it with grandchildren when they were old enough.

When my husband and I met 50+ years ago, we shared the love of nature and vowed someday to live on acreage of our own. We achieved that goal, and now live on and steward 160 acres of mostly forestland in the foothills of the Oregon Coast Range.

As a retired elementary school teacher, I have always loved sharing books with children. I hope this book will bring joy to adults and children alike, and that it will spur them on to explore Saddle Mountain or any other trail that beckons. — *Bonnie Shumaker*

About the Illustrator

Elecia Beebe grew up drawing and painting watercolors with parents who were artists themselves. Her artwork has illustrated View-Master reels and zoo literature, but this is her first time as illustrator for a children's book. Elecia was honored to be asked to do so by Bonnie Shumaker, who gave her daughter and so many other children in their small rural community a wonderful start in kindergarten and first grade. Elecia and her husband live down the road from Bonnie's farm and close to the magical Saddle Mountain trail.

Come visit us at:

www.palomabooks.com

Made in the USA
Las Vegas, NV
03 January 2022

39951361R00029